Take a Walk,
JOHNNY

Take a Walk, JOHNNY

Margaret Hillert

Illustrated by Yoshi Miyake

Follett Publishing Company

Editorial Offices: Chicago, Illinois

Regional Offices: Chicago, Illinois
Atlanta, Georgia • Dallas, Texas
Sacramento, California • Warrensburg, Missouri

Library of Congress Cataloging in Publication Data

Hillert, Margaret.
   Take a walk, Johnny.

   Summary: Johnny's summer morning walks, taken initially from boredom, become quite adventurous.
   I. Miyake, Yoshi.   II. Title.
PZ7.H558Tak   [E]   81-4044
ISBN 0-695-41625-1   AACR2
ISBN 0-695-31625-7 (pbk.)

28478

First Printing

During the school year Johnny got up early
every morning. He ate a good breakfast
and got dressed. Then he made his bed,
cleaned up his room, and went off to
school with his friends.

5

When summer came, school was out. Johnny got up early on the first day of summer. He ate a good breakfast and got dressed. Then he made his bed, cleaned up his room, and looked for something to do.

First Johnny played with his toy cars. Then he made silly faces in the mirror and laughed to see himself.

Next Johnny looked at the plants that were growing in the glass box on the table.

After that he went to his mother and said, "Mother, what can I do now? I don't have anything to do."

Mother said, "Take a walk, Johnny."

So Johnny went out to the yard and
walked around. He saw a bird up in a
tree. He saw a butterfly on a flower.
Then, under the flowers, he saw a big,
brown toad.

"Hello, toad!" said Johnny. "What a good
find you are! You have lots of bumps
and funny eyes. Don't jump away, toad.
I want to take you into the house and
show you to Mother. She'll be surprised!"

8

Johnny went into the house. "Mother, look
at this toad!" he said. "Isn't he great?"

"Yes," said Mother. "He's a fine-looking
toad. Why don't you put him into your
glass box with the plants? That would
be a good place for him."

The next morning Johnny made his bed, cleaned up his room, and looked for something to do.

First he fed the toad. Then he took the toad out of the box and let him hop around the room.

After that Johnny went to his mother and said, "Mother, what can I do now? I don't have anything to do."

Mother said, "Take a walk, Johnny."

Johnny went out to the yard with his toad. He put the toad back under the flowers.

"Good-bye, toad," said Johnny. "You'll be happier here."

Johnny walked down the sidewalk and looked all around. "I wonder what I'll find today," he said.

Then, under a tree, he saw a rock.

"What a pretty rock," said Johnny. "It has red and white spots, and it even seems to shine a little. I'll take it home and put it with my other rocks."

Johnny went back to his house. "Mother, look at this rock!" he said.

"It's a beautiful rock," said Mother. "I'm glad you found it. You can put it with your other rocks."

The next morning Johnny made his bed, cleaned up his room, and looked for something to do.

First he took out all his rocks. Then he put them all back in boxes again.

After that Johnny went to his mother and said, "Mother, what can I do now? I don't have anything to do."

Mother said, "Take a walk, Johnny."

Johnny went outside. "Take a walk. Take a walk," he said. "That's all I ever seem to do. But this time I know where I'll go."

Johnny walked to the library.

"Just look at all the books," he said. "I can get a book about almost anything. There are books about cowboys and wagons, bridges and mountains, and elephants and circuses. What a wonderful place this is!"

16

Johnny picked out some books and took
them home. "Look here, Mother," he said.
"I like to read, and these books are full of
good things to read about."

"I see you went to the library," said
Mother. "What a good idea! Books are
fun to read, and it looks like you found
some good ones."

The next morning Johnny made his bed, cleaned up his room, and looked for something to do.

He read for a time. Then he put all his books away.

After that Johnny went to his mother and said, "Mother, what can I do now? I don't have anything to do."

Mother said, "Take a walk, Johnny."

Johnny went outside and began to walk. "Walk, walk, walk," he said. "I'm getting tired of all this walking."

Suddenly he saw something shiny on the sidewalk. "What's this?" he said. "It's money right here on the sidewalk! Now I can **run** to the ice cream store."

So Johnny ran to the ice cream store.

"Boy, what a great place!" he said.
"Just look at all the different kinds of
ice cream. There are so many kinds that
I don't know which one to pick."

"Take your time," said the man.

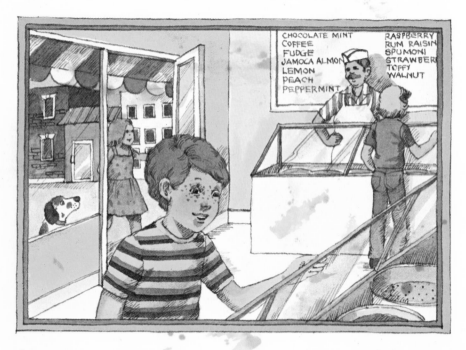

"The chocolate looks good," said Johnny
at last. "I would like a chocolate ice
cream cone."

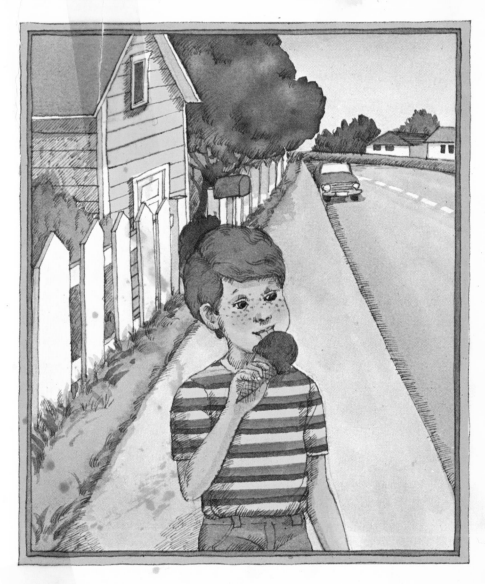

Johnny ate his ice cream cone on the way
home.

"Mother!" said Johnny. "Guess what I found on my walk this time. I found money! I found money, and I got an ice cream cone."

"You did?" said Mother. "The money was a good find, wasn't it?"

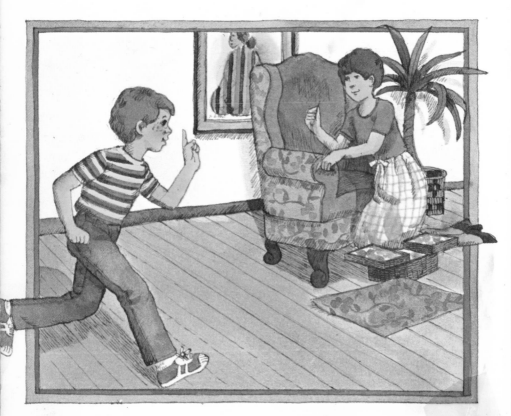

The next morning Johnny did all the
same things. He ate breakfast. He
made his bed. He cleaned up his room.

After that Johnny went to his mother and
said, "Mother, I am going for a walk."

His mother said, "Have a good time,
Johnny."

Johnny walked and walked and walked. He
walked up and down. He walked around
and around.

Suddenly Johnny saw a little puppy in the
street. "Here, puppy. Here, puppy," he called.

But the puppy did not move out of the
street.

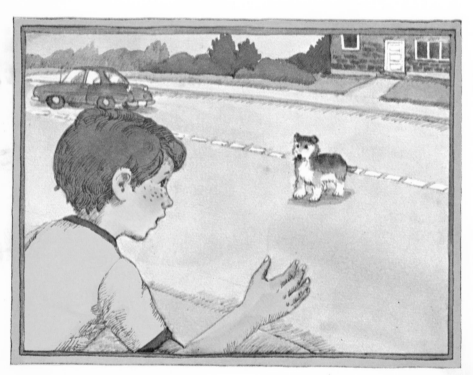

Johnny looked both ways for cars. Then he ran to get the puppy out of the street.

"Oh, you poor little thing," said Johnny. "Don't you have a home? You must be lost. I'll bet you need something to eat. Do you want to come home with me? Maybe I can keep you."

Johnny took the puppy home.

"Mother!" said Johnny. "Look what I found on my walk this time. She is so little. I think she is lost. May we keep her, Mother?"

"Well," said Mother. "First let's read the Lost and Found part of the newspaper."

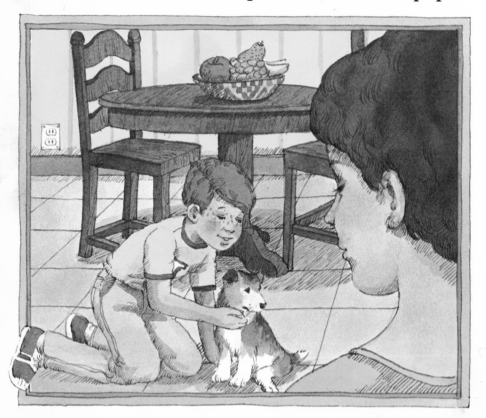

Mother looked in the newspaper. "No, I don't see anything about a lost puppy in here," she said. "Now we will make some signs."

Johnny and his mother made signs. The signs looked like this.

They put one sign on a tree. They put another sign in the ice cream store. When they got home, the telephone rang.

"I see you found my puppy," said a man on the telephone. "You can have her. I can't take care of her."

Mother told Johnny what the man had said. "You can keep the puppy, Johnny," said Mother. "She's as cute as a button."

28

"Cute as a button. Cute as a button," said Johnny. "Oh, Mother. Button would be a nice name for her."

Then Johnny called to the puppy. "Here, Button. Here, Button. Now you are my puppy. We'll be such good friends."

Every morning after that, Johnny got up early and ate a good breakfast. Then he made his bed, cleaned up his room, and went for a walk with Button.

And sometimes Mother went walking
with them.

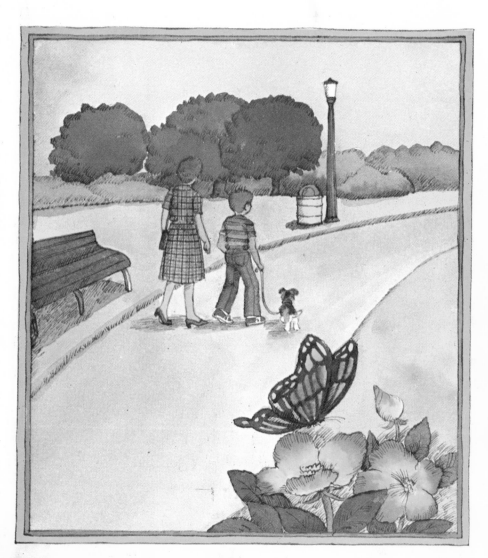

Margaret Hillert, author of many Follett JUST Beginning-To-Read Books, has been a first-grade teacher in Royal Oak, Michigan, since 1948.

In addition to giving practice with words that most children will recognize, *Take a Walk, Johnny* uses the 35 enrichment words listed below.

breakfast	dressed	nice	shine
bridges	during		shiny
bumps		outside	sidewalk
butterfly	early		signs
button	elephants	plants	spots
		poor	suddenly
chocolate	ice		
circuses	idea	rang	telephone
cone		rock(s)	tired
cowboys	mirror		toad
cream			
cute			wonder
			wonderful